KNOCK KNOCK
SUPERHERO

KNOCK
KNOCK

Caryl Hart & Nick East

HODDER CHILDREN'S BOOKS

First published in Great Britain in 2020 by Hodder and Stoughton

Text © Caryl Hart, 2020
Illustrations © Nick East, 2020

The moral rights of the author and illustrator have been asserted.

A CIP catalogue record of this book
is available from the British Library.

HB ISBN: 978 1 444 94593 5
PB ISBN: 978 1 444 94594 2

10 9 8 7 6 5 4 3 2 1

Printed and bound in China.

MIX
Paper from
responsible sources
FSC® C104740

Hodder Children's Books
An imprint of
Hachette Children's Group
Part of Hodder and Stoughton
Carmelite House
50 Victoria Embankment
London EC4Y 0DZ

An Hachette UK Company
www.hachette.co.uk

www.hachettechildrens.co.uk

Hodder
Children's
Books

KNOCK KNOCK
SUPERHERO

Caryl Hart & Nick East

ONE superhero's outside. **Wow!**
"Quick! Let me in!" he begs me. "Please . . ."

"Is your name Pasta Man?" I say.
"Why are you at my house today?"
He groans, "It's not my finest hour.
I've run right out of Pasta Power!"

"That's sad," I shrug. "But I can't help."

Then Pasta Man lets out a yelp.
"Oh NO!" he cries. "I have to hide!"
He pushes past and runs inside.

Just then, TWO Muscle Mums appear.
"Quick! Madame Chilli's coming near!
She's out to rule the world by force
With lashings of hot chilli sauce!"

SPLAT

WHIZZZZZZZZZZZ

ZIPPPPPPPP

THREE Glasses Girls all shout out, "Hey!
We saw you from six miles away.

We know exactly
what to do.
Quick! To the basement
— all of you!"

I see beside me
on the floor
A door that wasn't
there before.

The spiral stairs wind
round and round,
To a secret room,
deep underground . . .

CREAK

And there FOUR Gadget Grannies sit,
All testing gizmos while they knit.
"Oh, hello, dear! Put on your mask,
You'll need it for this dangerous task."

"My babysitter's here," I say.
"He won't like 'dangerous'. No way!"

FIVE Brainy Boys laugh, "Don't be scared.
You'll be all right. We're well prepared."

So . . . .

. . . we pull on capes
and flying boots,

NAAAR

magnetic gloves

BZZZT

and flame-proof suits.

ZZZIP

WHOOOOOSH

"Come quick!" the Boys cry. "Here we are!
Our Supersonic Supercar!"
We all squash in. The switches glow.
"To Meatball Mountain! Off we go!"

But . . .

SIX Boo-hoo Babies fight and squeal
And try to grab the steering wheel.
They cry so much, they flood the cave.
"Watch out!" I yell. "A tidal wave!"

The water churns.
The wipers swish.
I spot a whale, and lots of fish.
Then SEVEN Action Aunts swim by ...

And lift our car into the sky!

SPLOSH

Just then I see a UFO.
It's Madame Chilli! Help! Oh no!
"HEY! Give me all your gadgets, guys!
I'm going to **rule the world!"**
she cries.

EIGHT Stretchy Stepdads, all fantastic,
Ping past on bright-pink pants elastic.
They whisk us off into the night.
"Look, Meatball Mountain's now in sight!"

BOING
BOING

We park up on the crater's edge
Then inch along a narrow ledge,
Our faces lit up by the glow
Of bubbling Bolognese below.

Now Madame Chilli's closing in.

"Help! Pasta Man, don't let her win!"

But Pasta Man is tired and weak,

So feeble, he can hardly speak.

So down spaghetti ropes we slide, Towards the swirling sauce inside.

NINE Go-Go Grandpas cry, "Be quick! Some pasta sauce should do the trick!"

RUMBLE

But as we reach the mountain's core
Huge cracks appear across the floor.
The mountain is erupting . . . oh!
It isn't safe! We have to go!

RUM
RUM
RUM

Yay! TEN Super Sisters swoop
And save us from the steaming gloop!
They catch our dinner on the way.
"Now, eat it while it's hot," they say.

SLURP

So Pasta Man eats up his food
And – **look!** – his Pasta Power's renewed.

He lassoes naughty Madame Chilli
And tells her off for being silly.

We fly home in no time at all
And when I climb up to the hall,
My babysitter smiles, "Hello!
Your supper's ready — here you go.

Eat up and you'll be strong one day . . ."

"Oh, I already am!" I say.